This edition produced for St Martin's Press, New York in 1986 by
Octopus Books Limited
59 Grosvenor Street
London W1

© Gautier-Languereau 1976
© This translation Octopus Books Limited 1986

Library of Congress Cataloging in Publication Data
Ichikawa, Satomi.
Suzette and Nicholas in the garden.
Translation of: Suzette et Nicolas dans leur jardin.
Summary: Two children and their baby brother explore
the flower and vegetable gardens in their yard.
[1. Gardens—Fiction] I. Title.
PZ7.I16Su 1986   [E]   86–10194
ISBN 0–312–77982–8

Printed in Hong Kong

SATOMI ICHIKAWA

Suzette and Nicholas
IN THE GARDEN

St. Martin's Press/New York

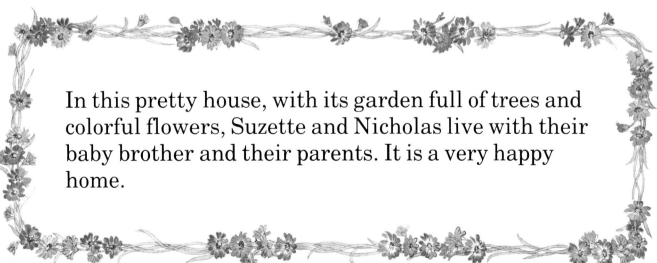

In this pretty house, with its garden full of trees and colorful flowers, Suzette and Nicholas live with their baby brother and their parents. It is a very happy home.

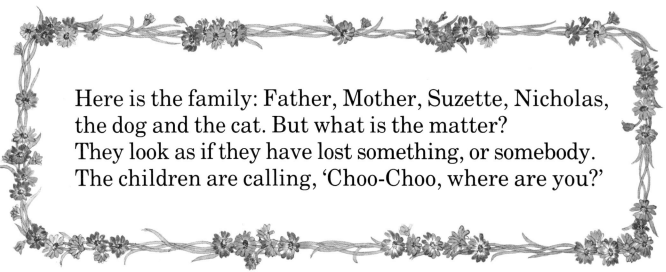

Here is the family: Father, Mother, Suzette, Nicholas,
the dog and the cat. But what is the matter?
They look as if they have lost something, or somebody.
The children are calling, 'Choo-Choo, where are you?'

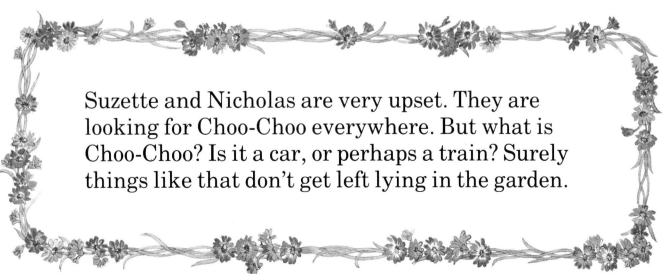

Suzette and Nicholas are very upset. They are looking for Choo-Choo everywhere. But what is Choo-Choo? Is it a car, or perhaps a train? Surely things like that don't get left lying in the garden.

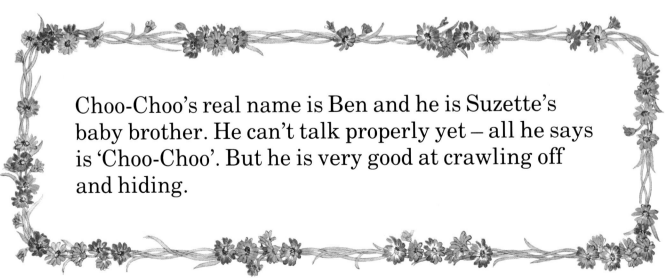

Choo-Choo's real name is Ben and he is Suzette's
baby brother. He can't talk properly yet – all he says
is 'Choo-Choo'. But he is very good at crawling off
and hiding.

Choo-Choo has been hiding behind a lilac tree, looking at a little bird sitting on a branch. Nicholas is so pleased to have found his brother that he isn't at all cross with him.

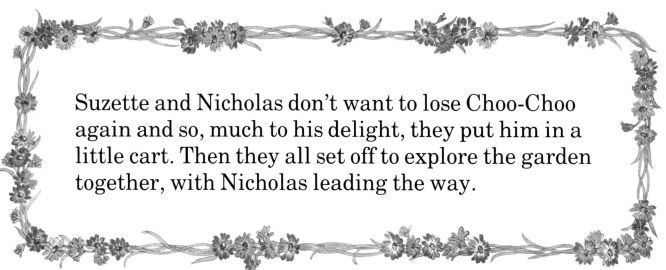

Suzette and Nicholas don't want to lose Choo-Choo
again and so, much to his delight, they put him in a
little cart. Then they all set off to explore the garden
together, with Nicholas leading the way.

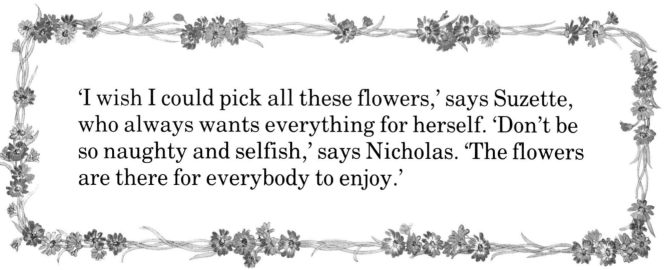

'I wish I could pick all these flowers,' says Suzette, who always wants everything for herself. 'Don't be so naughty and selfish,' says Nicholas. 'The flowers are there for everybody to enjoy.'

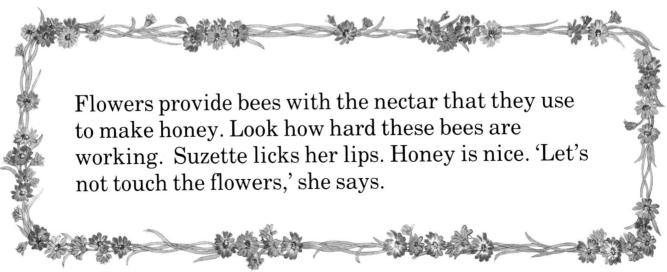

Flowers provide bees with the nectar that they use to make honey. Look how hard these bees are working. Suzette licks her lips. Honey is nice. 'Let's not touch the flowers,' she says.

Choo-Choo has found a pretty gray snail. He's holding it tightly in his fist. Nicholas tells him to let it go. 'It hasn't harmed anybody. It eats even less than Aunt Anna when she's dieting.'

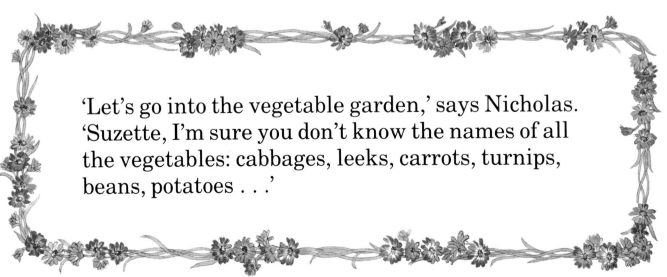

'Let's go into the vegetable garden,' says Nicholas.
'Suzette, I'm sure you don't know the names of all
the vegetables: cabbages, leeks, carrots, turnips,
beans, potatoes . . .'

'Stop it!' yells Suzette, putting her hands over her
ears. 'I hate vegetables. Let's go and say hello to the
goldfish instead. They look so sad going round and
round in their pond.'

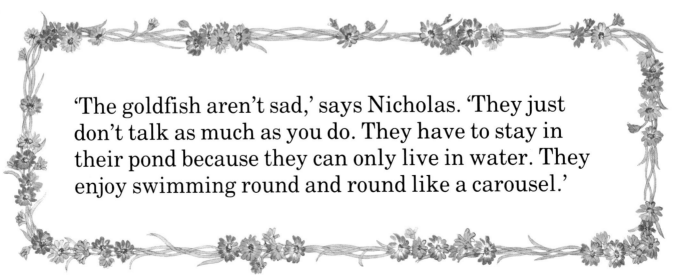

'The goldfish aren't sad,' says Nicholas. 'They just don't talk as much as you do. They have to stay in their pond because they can only live in water. They enjoy swimming round and round like a carousel.'

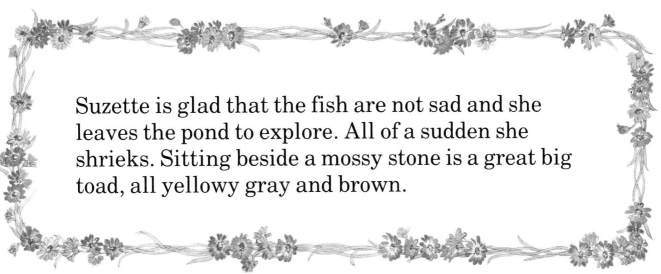

Suzette is glad that the fish are not sad and she leaves the pond to explore. All of a sudden she shrieks. Sitting beside a mossy stone is a great big toad, all yellowy gray and brown.

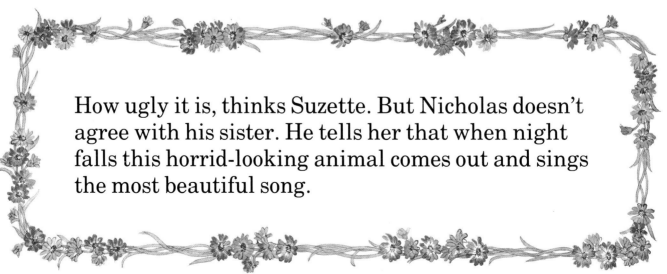

How ugly it is, thinks Suzette. But Nicholas doesn't agree with his sister. He tells her that when night falls this horrid-looking animal comes out and sings the most beautiful song.

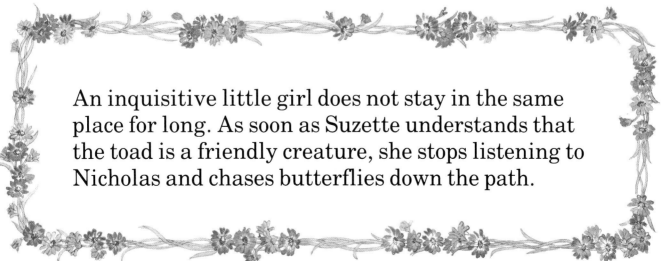

An inquisitive little girl does not stay in the same place for long. As soon as Suzette understands that the toad is a friendly creature, she stops listening to Nicholas and chases butterflies down the path.

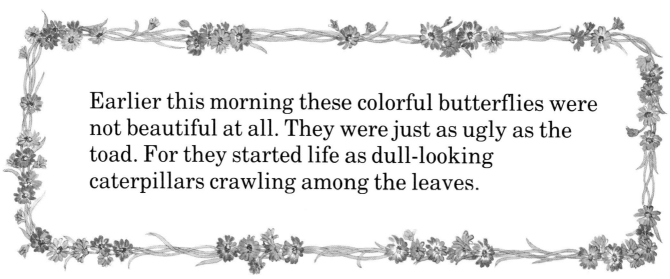

Earlier this morning these colorful butterflies were not beautiful at all. They were just as ugly as the toad. For they started life as dull-looking caterpillars crawling among the leaves.

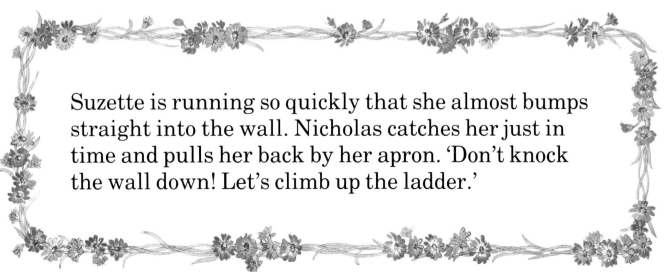

Suzette is running so quickly that she almost bumps straight into the wall. Nicholas catches her just in time and pulls her back by her apron. 'Don't knock the wall down! Let's climb up the ladder.'

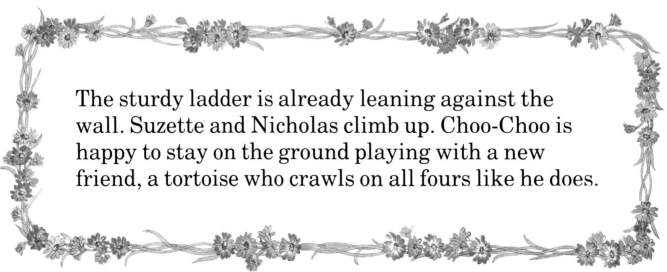

The sturdy ladder is already leaning against the wall. Suzette and Nicholas climb up. Choo-Choo is happy to stay on the ground playing with a new friend, a tortoise who crawls on all fours like he does.

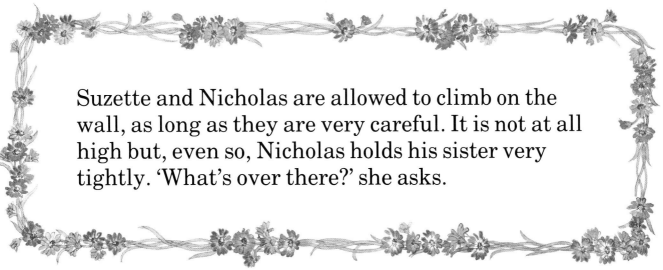

Suzette and Nicholas are allowed to climb on the
wall, as long as they are very careful. It is not at all
high but, even so, Nicholas holds his sister very
tightly. 'What's over there?' she asks.

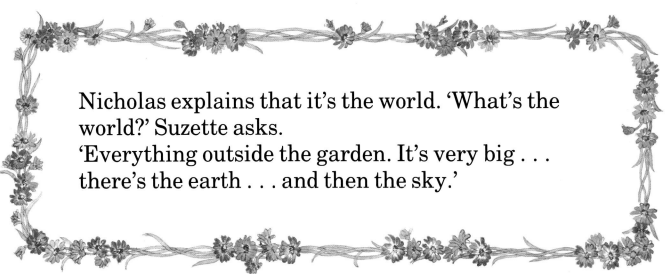

Nicholas explains that it's the world. 'What's the world?' Suzette asks.
'Everything outside the garden. It's very big . . . there's the earth . . . and then the sky.'

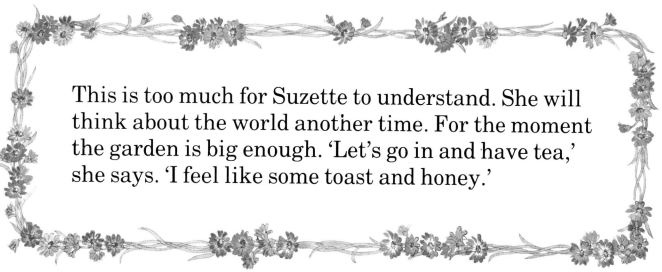

This is too much for Suzette to understand. She will think about the world another time. For the moment the garden is big enough. 'Let's go in and have tea,' she says. 'I feel like some toast and honey.'

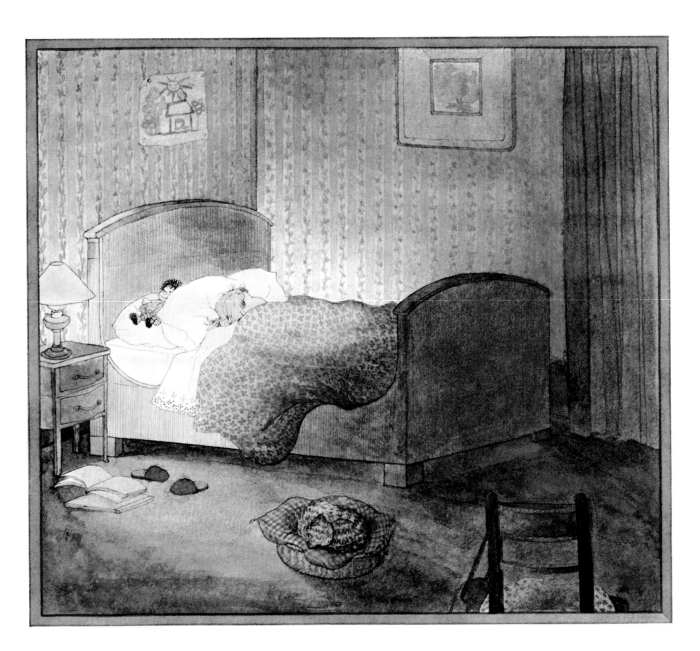

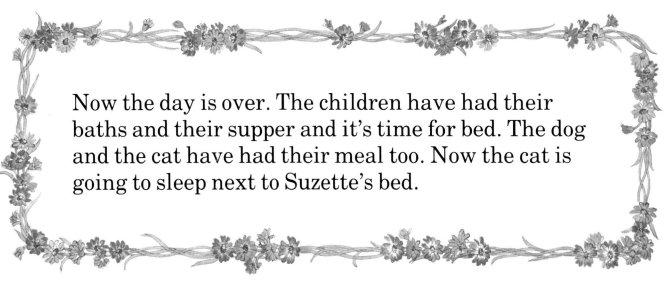

Now the day is over. The children have had their baths and their supper and it's time for bed. The dog and the cat have had their meal too. Now the cat is going to sleep next to Suzette's bed.

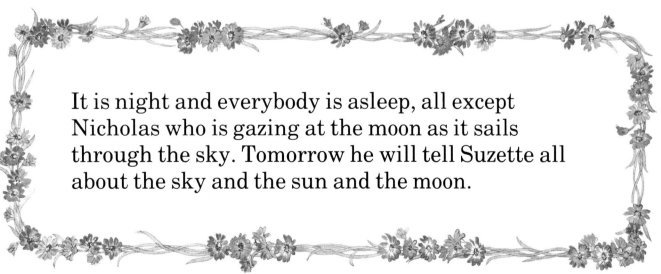

It is night and everybody is asleep, all except
Nicholas who is gazing at the moon as it sails
through the sky. Tomorrow he will tell Suzette all
about the sky and the sun and the moon.